Incy Wincy Spider

and friends

Miles Kelly

First published in 2011 by Miles Kelly Publishing Ltd
Harding's Barn, Bardfield End Green, Thaxted, Essex, CM6 3PX, UK

Copyright © Miles Kelly Publishing Ltd 2011

This edition printed in 2011

4 6 8 10 9 7 5 3

Editorial Director Belinda Gallagher
Art Director Jo Cowan
Editor Sarah Parkin
Cover/Junior Designer Kayleigh Allen
Production Manager Elizabeth Collins
Reprographics Stephan Davis, Ian Paulyn
Assets Lorraine King, Cathy Miles

ISBN 978-1-84810-413-6

Printed in China

British Library Cataloguing-in-Publication Data
A catalogue record for this book is available from the British Library

ACKNOWLEDGEMENTS

Artworks are from the Miles Kelly Artwork Bank
Cover artist: Kirsten Wilson

Made with paper from a sustainable forest

www.mileskelly.net
info@mileskelly.net
www.factsforprojects.com

Contents

Old Mother Hubbard

Old Mother Hubbard
Went to the cupboard
To get her poor dog a bone;
But when she came there
The cupboard was bare,
And so the poor dog had none.

As I was Going to St Ives

As I was going to St Ives,
I met a man with seven wives.
Each wife had seven sacks,
Each sack had seven cats,
Each cat had seven kits;
Kits, cats, sacks and wives,
How many were going to St Ives?

Peter, Peter

Peter, Peter, pumpkin-eater,
Had a wife and couldn't keep her;
He put her in a pumpkin shell,
And there he kept her very well.

High in the Pine Tree

High in the pine tree,
The little turtledove
Made a little nursery
To please her little love.

"Coo," said the turtledove,
"Coo," said she,
In the long shady branches
Of the dark pine tree.

The Ugly Duckling

A retelling from the original story
by Hans Christian Andersen

Mother duck was waiting for her eggs to hatch. Slowly the first shell cracked and a tiny bill and a little wing appeared. Then a yellow duckling fell out. Soon he stood beside his mother, watching as his sisters and brothers pushed their way out of their shells.

There was only one shell left. It was the largest, and mother duck wondered why it was taking so much longer than the others. There was a sudden crack, and there lay the biggest and ugliest duckling she had ever seen. His feathers were brown and grey.

"Oh dear," said mother duck.

She led the family down to the river, the ugly duckling trailing along behind the others. They splashed into the water and were soon swimming gracefully, all except the ugly duckling, who looked large and awkward even on the water.

"Oh dear," said mother duck.

The family set off for the farmyard where

they were greeted with hoots, moos, barks and snorts from the other animals.

"Whatever is that?" said the rooster, pointing at the ugly duckling. All the other ducklings huddled round their mother and tried to pretend the ugly duckling was not with them.

"Oh dear," said mother duck.

The ugly duckling felt sad and lonely. No one seemed to like him, so he ran away and hid in some dark reeds. Some hunters came by with their loud guns and fierce dogs. The ugly duckling paddled deeper into the reeds. Only later in the day, as it was growing dark, did the ugly duckling stir from his hiding place.

All summer he wandered over fields and down rivers. Everywhere

he went people laughed at him, and other ducks he met just hissed at him. As well as being ugly, the duckling was lonely and unhappy. Soon winter came and the rivers began to freeze over. One day the duckling found himself trapped in the ice. He tucked his head under his wing, and decided that his short life must have come to an end.

He was still there early the next morning when a farmer came by. The farmer broke the ice and wrapped the ugly duckling in his jacket, then carried him home to his children. They put the ugly duckling in a box by the fire, and fed him and stroked his feathers. There the ugly duckling stayed through the winter, growing bigger all the time.

The farmer's wife never had much time for the ugly duckling. He was always getting under her feet in the kitchen, and he was so clumsy that he kept knocking things over. One day, the farmer's wife chased the ugly duckling out of her kitchen, out of the farmyard and through the gate down the lane.

It was a perfect spring day. The apple trees were covered in blossom, the grass was green and the air was filled with the sound of birdsong. The ugly duckling wandered down to the river, and there he saw three magnificent white swans. They were so beautiful and graceful as they glided towards the bank where he stood.

He waited for them to hiss at him and beat the water with their wings to frighten him away, but they didn't do any such thing. Instead they called him to come and join them. At first he thought it was a joke, but they asked him again.

He bent down to get into the water, and

there was his reflection. But where was the ugly duckling? All he could see was another magnificent swan. Not an ugly duckling, but a swan. He lifted his long neck, and called in sheer delight, "I am a SWAN!" and he sailed over the water to join his real family.

Incy Wincy Spider

Incy Wincy Spider
Climbed up the water spout;
Down came the rain
And washed the spider out,
Out came the sun
And dried up all the rain;
So Incy Wincy Spider
Climbed up the spout again.

Use your fingers to
be the spider climbing
up the spout.

Wriggle your fingers
to be the rain.

Sweep your hands in an
arch to show the sun.

Use your fingers to be
the spider climbing back
up the spout.

Sing a Song of Sixpence

Sing a song of sixpence,
A pocket full of rye;
Four-and-twenty blackbirds
Baked in a pie.

When the pie was opened
The birds began to sing;
Was not that a dainty dish
To set before the king?

The king was in his counting-house
Counting out his money;
The queen was in the parlour
Eating bread and honey.

The maid was in the garden
Hanging out the clothes,
When down came a blackbird,
And pecked off her nose.

Girls and Boys

Girls and boys, come out to play,
The moon doth shine as bright as day;
Leave your supper and leave your sleep,
And come with your playfellows
into the street,

Come with a whoop,
Come with a call,
Come with a good will
Or come not at all.

Rain, Rain

Rain, rain, go away,
Come again another day;
Little Tommy wants to play.

Simple Simon

Simple Simon met a pieman,
Going to the fair;
Says Simple Simon to the pieman,
"Let me taste your ware."

Says the pieman to Simple Simon,
"Show me first your penny."
Says Simple Simon to the pieman,
"Indeed I have not any."

Over the Hills

Tom, he was a piper's son,
He learned to play
when he was young,
And all the tune
that he could play
Was 'over the hills
and a great way off,
The wind shall blow
my top knot off'.

Dance to your Daddy

Dance to your daddy,
My bonnie laddy,
Dance to your daddy,
my bonny lamb.

You shall get a fishy,
On a little dishy,
You shall get a fishy when
the boat comes home.

Dance to your daddy,
My bonnie laddy,
Dance to your daddy,
And to your mammy sing.

You shall get a coatie,
And a pair of breekies,
You shall get a coatie when
the boat comes in.

Little Red Riding Hood

There was once a little girl who lived in the middle of a deep, dark forest with her mother and father, who was a woodcutter. The little girl always wore a red cloak with a hood, and so she was called Little Red Riding Hood.

One day she decided to visit her granny who lived some way from the woodcutter's cottage. She took a basket with a cake her mother had baked and set off. Now the last thing her mother had said to Little Red Riding Hood was, "Don't leave the path, and don't talk to any strangers." But Little Red Riding Hood was not really listening.

So when she saw some bluebells growing
under a tree, she left the path and began to
pick a bunch for her granny. Slowly, slowly
she wandered further away from the path,
deeper into the trees. Suddenly, she was not
alone. There in front of her stood a great
big wolf. Now Little Red Riding Hood had
not met a wolf before so she did not realize
that wolves are not the kind of animals to

be too friendly with.

"Good day, little girl," said the wolf with a snarly sort of a smile. "What is your name and where are you going?"

"My name is Little Red Riding Hood. I am going to visit my granny, and I am taking her a cake to eat," replied Little Red Riding Hood.

The wolf was delighted. Not only a little girl to eat but a granny and a cake as well!

"And where does your granny live, little girl?" asked the wolf, trying hard to smile nicely despite his fierce teeth.

Little Red Riding Hood told the wolf where her granny lived, and went on picking bluebells. The wolf slipped away through the trees and soon found granny's cottage. He tapped on the door and said, in a disguised voice, "Hello, granny. It is Little Red Riding Hood. I have brought you a cake, will you let me in?"

As soon as the door was open, the wolf bounded in and gobbled the granny all up! He put on her nightcap and shawl and climbed into her bed. Soon he heard Little Red Riding Hood coming and he tried his snarly smile again.

"Hello, granny," said Little Red Riding Hood. "I have brought you a cake and these bluebells," and she came up to the bedside.

"Goodness, granny! What great big eyes you have!" she said.

"All the better to see you with," growled the wolf.

Little Red Riding Hood could not help

noticing the wolf's teeth.

"Goodness, granny! What great big teeth you have!"

"All the better to eat you with!" snapped

the wolf and gobbled Little Red Riding
Hood up. He gobbled up the cake in the
basket as well and then, very full indeed, he
fell fast asleep, snoring loudly.

Now by great good luck,
Little Red Riding Hood's
father was passing by the
cottage, and when he
heard the terrible
snores he put his head
round the door to see
who was making such a
noise. He was horrified
to see the wolf so he
took his axe and made
a great slit down the
wolf's tummy. Out
jumped Little Red Riding
Hood. Out staggered granny.
She stitched up the wolf's

tummy and told him to mind his manners
in future. Then, as there was no cake left for
tea, they all went back home, and Little
Red Riding Hood's mother made

pancakes. Little Red Riding Hood had
learnt her lesson, and she never spoke to
wolves again.

Hickory, Dickory, Dock

Hickory, dickory, dock,
The mouse ran up the clock.
The clock struck one,
The mouse ran down,
Hickory, dickory, dock.

One, Two, Buckle my Shoe

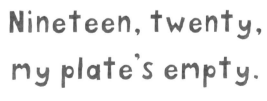

One, two, buckle my shoe,
Three, four, knock at the door,
Five, six, pick up sticks,
Seven, eight, lay them straight,
Nine, ten, a big fat hen,
Eleven, twelve, dig and delve,
Thirteen, fourteen, maids a-courting,
Fifteen, sixteen, maids in the kitchen,
Seventeen, eighteen, maids in waiting,
Nineteen, twenty,
my plate's empty.

Six Little Mice

Six little mice sat down to spin;
Pussy passed by and she peeped in.
"What are you doing, my little men?"
"Weaving coats for gentlemen."

"Shall I come in and cut off your threads?"
"No, no, Mistress Pussy,
you'd bite off our heads."
"Oh, no, I'll not, I'll help you to spin."
"That may be so, but you don't come in."

Hickety, Pickety

Hickety, pickety, my black hen,
She lays eggs for gentlemen;
Gentlemen come every day
To see what my black hen doth lay.
Sometimes nine and sometimes ten,
Hickety, pickety, my black hen.

Rock-a-bye Baby

Rock-a-bye baby,

On the tree top.

When the wind blows

The cradle will rock;

When the bough breaks

The cradle will fall.

Down will come baby,

Cradle and all.